LATEST EDITION

THE WORLD WITH IN

THE OTHER-WORLDLY ADVENTURE OF CHAD SMITH

Contents

Chapter 1

The Rejection that Lead to Discovery

It was one of those cloudy days at the bay. A not-so-warm wind was blowing in from the ocean. The tide had gone out, and the beach was strewn with kelp and stranded sea creatures. The seagulls were scarfing them up as fast as they could gobble them down. Every so often, the tide in this portion of the Pacific exceeds its retreat from the former days. It had gone way out this time. The moon had come closer to the Earth than it had in months, and its pull was strong. Chad had had a bad day at school. Since moving to the Bay Area, no new friends have come into his life. He hated it. The kids all had little clicks and stuck to each other like glue. He had tried to weasel his way into several of them but was always defeated. Today, he thought he had finally made it. Gertrude, the second most brilliant student in school, had sat across the table from him at lunch. Somehow, the topic got turned to his photographic memory. She wanted proof. So, she asked him a question to test it out.

"What was I wearing a month ago today?" She thought she had him for sure on that. Was she ever surprised?

"Let me see, today would have been April 24, one month ago. You were wearing a black sweater you purchased from JC Pennies for $39.98. It was on sale. You had jeans that matched it in color, and the top under your sweater had lavender flowers with green leaves and a pink ribbon around their stems; the print was a bouquet of flowers, lilacs to be exact."

"I know that top. How did you know I purchased the sweater at JC Pennies, though?"

"It said so on the price tag. You should have removed it before putting the sweater on."

It was hanging down in the back

above your behind, saying, 'Sale, $39.98.' It was like a tail on your..." He didn't have time to finish because she reached across the table and slapped him before abruptly getting up and leaving. She blurted out these words as she left.

"And to think about the time I started thinking you were an ok guy, I find out you are a pervert. You were looking at my ass, thinking to yourself it is for sale. Well, it isn't, not to the likes of you, at least." Slamming his fist down on the table, Chad muttered these words under his breath.

I was not watching your ass and thinking it was for sale. I was only looking at the price tag hanging from your sweater." Of course, she never heard that because she was long gone by then. Then there was the day earlier when Owen sat across from him at the same table. He was upset because Webber had told the class that day that half of the test would be based on Chapter 32 and the other half on his lecture. Owen had been absent that day, so how could he know what was said in the lecture? Chad then proceeded to repeat it word for word, even using the same inflection in his voice as the professor. It was really an impressive feat when you get right down to the facts. But did he get even a thank you from Owen? Nope! The guy got up and walked away, repeating some of the critical points he thought would be good to get seated more permanently in his mind. So, being the smartest kid in school did not help his social life at all. Geniuses like him only came around every few thousand students. He never had to study like the average kid. Whether it was a textbook or a computer program, it did not matter. All he had to do was see it once, and he had it. Likewise, he remembered all the lectures the teachers gave every word of them. You could not put anything over on him. He could have aced every quiz or test if he chose to do so. He had more knowledge about more things than any of his teachers. School was so dull for him he didn't know what to do most of the time. So, Chad fooled everyone and played dumb. If you somehow managed to converse with him, you would pass him off as a bit on the odd side. He was not only bizarre but acted the part when he wanted to, and that was about all the time now. It seemed like someone so smart could outsmart the clicks and wiggle his way into their inner circle, but alas, it was not to be. He did not possess the social skills to get along with people. That was the real problem. You can be the smartest kid within a hundred miles and still flunk out regarding social skills. It had nothing to do with his looks, either. If you passed him in the street, nothing about him would stand out except his hair. No matter what he did to it, it always did its own thing.

He was strolling along the beach with nothing in mind but to pass some time away from everybody. His feet made that crunching sound as he traipsed over the gravel. Occasionally, you might hear a crackle when he stepped on a dried air sack from some shriveled seaweed. He was making significant progress when he noticed

a rather large pool farther out past the beach where something had scooped the gravel. This was at least the third time he had been this way, and he never remembered seeing it before. He estimated it to be about five feet deep in the middle. Usually, this area would be covered in water, but not today. Seven large rocks formed a perfect circle in this larger-than-normal tide pool. The uncanny thing about it was the rocks were all about the same size like they had been arranged that way deliberately by someone or something. The boulders were too large for any five people to move, so it would have to be done with a machine. Perhaps a mini-excavator or skid-steer had done it at such a time as this when the tide was exceptionally far out to sea. It would have been tricky, though. A machine would have needed to be ready, and the operator would have had to calculate his timing precisely, or it could have gotten stuck there when the tide came back in.

Smith made his way over the

scattered seaweed and came up to the edge of the water surrounding the rocks. He looked at the area closely. It was a strange thing to behold, indeed. The sun showed through an opening in the clouds for just a moment, and he saw something shiny right in the middle of the circle. The golden light coming from it was very bright. Little streamers or lines radiated out from it, dazzling his eyes. Have you spent some time on the coast? You know how slimy sea water can feel on your skin, especially if it has a bunch of kelp. Chad knew and did not want to wade out in five feet of water and dive into it. That was the last thing on his mind now. He decided to see if he could glimpse the strange object from another angle. With his photographic memory, he took a mental picture of all the smaller rocks around the shiny thing. It was just in time because the clouds closed the gap, and the what-cha-ma-call-it winked out of sight.

Chad found the same group of rocks on the other side of the tide pool and peered through the water. There it was. He could just catch a glimpse of something in the center that was not natural. Whatever it was, it had been made by intelligent life. Perhaps it was a portion of a pop can. However, if that were the case, it was a small pop or juice can. He was about to return to the shore when some uncontrolled urge came over him. His curiosity overcame the dreaded water. As he started toward the circle's center, the ocean felt wet and surprisingly cold. It first came up to his ankles, soon to his knees, then his waist. He had reached one of the larger rocks. He did not want to touch it. It was covered with barnacles and crustaceans. Little sea anemia were waving their arms in rhythm with the currents that jetted around it. He could slip between the rocks if he were careful. There was just enough room. Now, the water was up to his shoulders. Twenty feet away, under some sea foam-covered kelp, was the middle. He took three deep breaths and dived under. In short order, his senses told him he had gone the proper distance. He would need to open his eyes to see for sure. You know what that meant, salt water in his eyes. At first, it is hard to get used to. It smarts sometimes, and you need to overcome the uncomfortable sensation it causes. But was a juice can all he would see when he opened his eyes? This circular thing was there just beyond the reach of his outstretched hand. If it was a juice can, someone must have cut the top and the bottom off because it had neither.

Soon, Chad had it in his hand. He approached the water's surface and paddled toward the two rocks he had passed through. Then he saw it. A giant jellyfish had taken up residence between them. This was not good. He dodged to the left and found the same. After paddling around the complete circle of rocks, he found a large jellyfish stationed between each of the openings blocking his retreat; seven openings, with seven jellyfish, and like the rocks, were all about the same size.

Jellyfish can numb a person if their tentacles touch bare skin. He was trapped. This was the oddest thing that had ever happened to him. He ran the calculations through his mastermind. The chance of this happening was about 9 to the tenth power. He couldn't believe it. They were protecting something, the something he now carried in his hand. Without thinking, he shoved it into his back pocket. It felt hard and cold next to his butt. The sea creatures did not budge an inch or give up their defensive position. There was only one option left. He had to climb up on one of those slimy rocks. He needed to go over them if he couldn't go under the jellyfish or through them. He chose his rock and, by pressing off the bottom, found that he could get his waste out of the water. He would then need to grab onto the rock and hoist himself up and over. He took three more breaths, then went down in a squatting position under the water in front of the rock and gave a mighty push with his legs. Then he was grasping the top of the slimy thing. In minutes, he was over and on the other side. He wasted no time in exiting the area. He wanted to get as far away from the place as he could.

An asphalt path ran parallel to the bay. He would pass the driftwood piles and start running once there. He would run all the way home if necessary. Someone had collected a bunch of driftwood and made a shelter there on the shore a long time ago. He could tell some time had passed because part of the structure had collapsed. Right in front of it was a large stump that had washed up on the beach. Somehow, it had managed to stay upright with its roots down like they should be, or at least what was left of the roots. He decided to sit on top to look at this strange object closer. The sun came out again and started drying the water on his skin. Then, the sticky itching started. It would be there until he showered.

Chapter 2

The Translucent Midget

The tube was just off round. Only an eye as trained as his would notice it, though. It was hollow and about 4 inches long. He could look through it. If he did so at the water, the thing acted like a polarizer lens on a camera. The light reflections on the water vanished if he twisted it one way and reappeared if he kept turning it around. It had engravings on the outside and a rim, like the rim of a can on either end. It was silver in color. Rainbow patterns had formed on the outside of it but not on the inside. At one end, it was purple, the other green. The colors swirled with reds, oranges, and some blues and yellows. It was like a rainbow had been captured on the surface. The markings were foreign to Chad. He had never seen anything like them. As his hand closed completely around the object, something unusual happened. A ring of thin film formed right in the center. It looked exactly like the soap created in a bubble ring's circle before you blow on it to make bubbles. Not knowing what else to do, he blew on it, half expecting some giant bubble to emerge from the center, but no such luck. He decided to look through it again. Before his hand had closed completely around it, there was nothing in the middle. He could see right through it. What would he see now looking through this thin lens? He pointed it at the circle of rocks and was amazed. Right in the center of the rocks where this object had been underwater, there appeared to be a fountain of water that shot into the sky. It was in motion-a living thing like a stream of water would look. Only this fountain kept going higher and higher. It looked like a shimmering glass tube that rose into the air and disappeared into the clouds. He swung all around, looking through the lens, but no other fountains were coming out

disappeared. He looked for the spout of water coming out of the center of the tide pool, but it was gone. Closing his fingers again, the lens sprang back into position. There was something about the electrical current in his body passing through his hand that caused it to form or dissipate. He was about to leave for home when he tried one more thing. Closing his fingers around the object again, he looked at the center of the driftwood structure. There appeared to be a strange little man in there beaconing for him to come. He was waving his tiny hands in the come motion. Chad looked at the pile of wood without the lens, and there was no little man there. It was empty. The man was there again when he looked through the scope. The little one jumped down from the stump and made his way slowly toward him. He was dressed like a semitransparent leprechaun. There were no colors in or on him. He was as transparent as the tube of seawater shooting into the heavens. The man was saying something. Chad could only read his lips. He was asking for help. The genius made his way to the driftwood pile. There was no substance there. If he was not looking through the lens, there was nothing. With it, however, he could see the guy plainly. The little man started to move out from under the shelter, beaconing Chad to follow. This he did.

In time, they entered a transparent tube like a culvert. Without the scope, Smith could see nothing. The edges evaporated. Looking through the scope, he saw it all. The tunnel grew larger and larger. Soon, he was able to stand up and walk. It was not a straight tunnel but weaved in and out. It went up over the asphalt path and continued between two houses. At one point, it went between two horses in a pasture. Chad was surprised that the fence inside of the tunnel had disappeared. He could pass right through it rather than needing to climb over it. Neither of the horses budged as he passed between them. A girl was riding in the pasture about a hundred feet away.

Chad went right by her, and she never saw him.

He was following, always following the little man. Then, the tunnel did the impossible. It went down into the ground. Once inside the earth, he could put the scope away. It was no longer needed. It was also dark in there, but the little man appeared like a luminescent lantern as he moved forward. Finally, they came to a large room. There was a rainbow film covering the entrance that looked ever so much like the lens inside of the scope he carried. Chad stopped short. The little one passed through the film and continued beaconing him forward. He took three deep breaths and made the plunge. Immediately, he could hear. Chad looked around and saw a tiny fireplace with flames devouring some small pieces of coal. He could feel the heat of it. The little man led him to a chair next to the fire and told him to be seated. The giant hardly fit on it. His cheeks overhung on each side then the little one talked.

He spoke perfect English but with a strong South African accent. He was, all in all, about three feet tall. Upon closer examination, the miniature man was not a leprechaun at all but a very tiny, human-looking creature. He did not have the pointed ears one would expect on such a little person.

"Scoot your chair a little closer to the fire. It will help dry your clothes. All the minerals and salty grime were filtered away when you passed through the door. Your wet clothes are wet with pure, clean water." Chad could sense that now since this little thing had pointed it out to him. He felt clean all over, like a spring rain had come out of the heavens and washed him all over. He looked closer at the little man when he started speaking again.

"I expect you have a lot of questions, Chad," the little voice spoke as the one it came from found his own seat on the other side of the fireplace.

"How do you know my name?"

"We know all about you. We have been watching you struggle with your

new school. We directed you to come

"Why me? And why we," questioned the lad? "You mean to say there is more than one of you?" The little man rubbed the beard on his chin and lifted both hands up as if in a gesture of defeat before answering.

"Why, you? We know of your exceptional mind and need your help, and yes, there are more of us. There are thousands of us. We have lived here by this bay for centuries. We were here before the Indians came. Our race goes back a very long time."

"Why have you been watching me?" Chad took the little scope out of his pocket and started to make the circle with his fingers again.

"Stop, do not activate the ring down here, please!" The little guy spoke desperately as he moved his hands back and forth wildly while shaking his head no.

"Why not? What is this thing anyway, and why was it there in the exact center of the rocks? Also, what is that ring that appears in the middle when I close my fingers entirely around it? I thought it was like a soap film in a can of bubbles. I tried to make a bubble with it, but nothing happened." The miniature one looked deep into the eyes of the kid genius for several seconds as if pondering his answer, then spoke.

"You must not close your fingers around the ring in here because it will make too much noise. My people do not know that you have come yet. It is not time to let them know. I need to share some things with you before you meet them. You asked what the ring tube was. It is called a 'polarscoptic resonator.' It allows you to see into our world. Why were you directed to come here? Our race is in big trouble. We need you to help us. An ancient rival has broken through our cloaking technology and is determined to force us to join them in a war against humanity. If this were to happen, your people up there would be in grave danger. You would have to fight an invisible enemy. They would come at you from all directions, and you could never see them. Millions of you would be slaughtered." Chad was getting a little bit concerned now as he pondered the things the small man had just shared with him.

"What is your name?"

"I go by the name of Rex. Our names are like yours in most cases. We speak your language. We have adapted your lifestyle. We have technologies just as you do. We have vehicles and means of travel that allow us to go from pole to pole in a matter of minutes only we go underground, and you go through the air."

"What do you mean traveling from pole to pole in a matter of minutes? The fastest jetliner would take hours to make that flight." Chad waved the tube back and forth to emphasize his statement. Rex started waving his little hands again and shaking his head NO to cause him to stop moving it around.

"Your people have the vehicles. They have hundreds of them, but few of your kind know this." Chad started to put the ring in his pocket when Rex hopped up from his chair and came over with a small leather case that fit the tube exactly. It had some precious stones arranged in an exotic design attached to the middle and ends. A zipper less zipper went around in a circle to open a cap at the top. Once the thing was inside the pouch, Rex relaxed a great deal and continued speaking. "About it making a bubble? Yes, it can. You need to place both hands around it, ensuring that both fingers are touching; then, if you blow through it, a giant bubble will form. You can then enter into the bubble, and when it pops, you will be back in our world, THE WORLD WITHIN. You could do this in chemistry class if you ever had to. The other kids would see you enter the bubble, then poof; you would vanish when it popped. In fact, next week, your teacher will be talking about soap bubbles and their concentration." After listening to this information, Chad blurted out the remaining questions that were uppermost in his mind.

"What was that strange circle

of rocks, and why was there a tube of water going up into the heavens? I could not see it naturally, but it was there when I looked through the polar resonator. And why were the jellyfish blocking my retreat from the center of the rocks? The little man appeared to turn white. The blood drained from his face, if he had any blood. He found his tiny chair and seated himself again. Finally, he spoke but did not answer the questions right away.

"You mean to say there is a tube of water going into the heavens from the sea?"

"Yes, I saw that when I activated the scope and looked in the circle's center. Why is that a problem?" Smith was concerned now that Rex was so concerned.

"That means they are already here. It is a miracle you managed to escape from the middle of the rocks. And you really saw the jellyfish? Were they actually blocking your way out between the rocks? You didn't look back over your shoulder, did you? Of course, you didn't, or you wouldn't be here with me now. You would be somewhere in the Atlantic Ocean. Dear me! This is very grave news, very grave indeed! Come with me, Chad, quickly! I need to show you some things before we talk with the Matriarch. She will need to call a meeting immediately with our defense minister."

Chapter 3

Electronic Vaccination

The kid genius followed Rex into another room. This one was larger than the one with the fireplace. It had a little kitchen where food was prepared. Chad wondered what these little people ate. If they existed in a different dimension than the one earthling's lived in, was there a different kind of food within this world? He didn't have long to wait. A tiny cat came in and rubbed up against his shoe. It was dry now. There was not even any salt water sloshing around inside as there had been just a few minutes ago. Over on a small counter was something that looked like a tiny chicken plucked and ready to be prepared for a meal. So these little people had little animals and birds that, like Rex, were miniature replicas of the world.

A tiny refrigerator in the room also had a freezer door on top. They had the equivalent of electricity with small cords going into outlet plugs. Chad heard a steady beat coming from the other side of the wall on his right. Rex saw him looking around as if reading his mind confirmed what the boy was thinking.

"Our technologies are like yours in most cases except the power source. You power your electricity with dams, wind generators, solar panels, coal plants, petroleum products, and the like. We, however, tap into the magnetic force field of the earth. There was another genius who lived long before your time. You know his name. It is Tesla. He was so far ahead of his time that few realized his genius. Your people passed him off as nothing. His inventions would have transformed your world into a far better management of the resources Mother Earth had provided. The oil tycoons, though, did not want to lose their edge. Oil was your world's currency, so they squelched his brilliance because of greed. We actually were his inspiration. We shared our knowledge with him, but it was too early; the world without was not ready.

Now, however, it is moving into a position to take advantage of forms of power that do not deplete the planet's resources. Not that that is a problem, really. There are enough resources beneath the earth's surface to power her population for thousands and thousands of years. Your people in power do not want to let go of their greed. That is the problem. You, Chad, will help change all that if you will work with us to solve our immediate problem. Once our race is secure, we will share with you many wonders. You will have the potential to make billions and billions of dollars. Will you help us?" Chad had been listening to the little man closely while he was talking. Had he wanted to, he could have repeated this little speech word for word. He had quickly grasped the complete meaning of what Rex had stated.

"What exactly do you want me to help you with? I still haven't figured that out from our brief conversations."

"We want you to help us put encryption on our cloaking system so the Sea Surrogates cannot infiltrate our people and cause us to go to war with humanity." Chad knew quite a bit about encryption for a kid. He could have chatted with the world's best encryption specialists and not sounded ignorant about the process. A lot of thoughts started racing through his enlarged brain.

"Who are the Sea Surrogates," he asked quickly as he stifled a sneeze that was coming on. Chad was allergic to cats, but since this one was so small, it took quite a while for him to be affected. "Are they a race of small humans such as you?" The little man was slightly offended by Chad calling his people a race of tiny humans. In the first place, they were not humans, biologically speaking, although they looked like them. In the second place, he was offended that the lad considered them small. He regained his composure before answering the question, however.

"We are not small humans, Chad. Our biological makeup is not like yours. We have a circulatory system, but it is not blood that runs through it; it is electrical current. Though our food looks like yours, it is also made of substantive energy. We do not grow old and die. We are immortals. New beings come into existence but not through a birth process like your own. We propagate by asexual means." Smith knew about that type of reproduction. They were studying it in his biology class. As he thought of the name Sea-Surrogate, the concept of who this other race of beings was flashed through his mind. He assumed the name Surrogate would mean that a group of rival dwellers from the world within could have commandeered the asexual reproduction process of the little humanoids and was mass producing them through some form of Cloning process using a surrogate host.

Furthermore, Rex's race was seeking his help to encrypt their current electrical makeup so that the Surrogates could no longer mass-produce copies of them. His assumptions were right on target. Rex saw the evidence of this understanding and smiled for the first time. The kid genius noted that he had teeth even as did their human counterparts.

"So, you will help us defeat our rivals; I see it in your eyes. This is excellent news. How do you propose to do this?" Chad was way ahead of him. He felt this quest could be accomplished by mass electrical vaccination. Where humans would require a biological type of vaccine, these humanoids would require a vaccination electrical in nature. Part of the process of making that vaccine would require some form of encryption as part of the whole. Their electrical makeup would be altered to prevent any meddling from outside races of like beings.

"Do you want to wipe your enemies from existence?" When he heard it, the little man looked horrified at such a thought. Was that even possible? And no, it was not their intent to eliminate them, only curb their intrusion into the affairs of his people.

"No, not at all! We do not want to eliminate them; we want to return our relations to what they were before the breach. Our races trade with each other. We have done so for millennia. While they are dwellers of the sea, we are dwellers of the earth. They have the resources we need. Likewise, we have elements they need." Chad spoke again after pondering Rex's response.

"I think I will need to create a double electronic vaccination. There will be one for your race and one for theirs. Your people will take it voluntarily; their people will get it whether they want to or not." Rex grew very excited. None of their leaders had ever thought of an injection that would solve their dilemma. Chad continued: "Do you want the clones they have produced from your race to join you? What is to become of them?" Rex thought about it. He had a little beard that he loved twisting in his fingers. He did that now, as he answered.

"That is an excellent question. We will need to talk to Her Majesty about it. A lot depends on how many of us they have produced and what they are doing with them. Do they even have a soul? And by the way, your suggestion of an injection is pure genius. I do not think that has ever crossed our minds."

"What would you do with them if you found out they had no soul?"

"I expect we would not want them with us."

"Then we may need to manufacture a third vaccine that will transform them into the form of their creators. By the way, what form are the Sea-Surrogates in? You have not shared that with me yet." In response, Rex opened one of the kitchen cabinet drawers and pulled out a small photo album.

Chapter 4

The Electronoyd's Dilemma

Chad's mom was worried. Her son had yet to return from his stroll along the beach. Supper had grown cold, and the sun was setting. She watched out the window as it sunk behind the water. It had not been an easy life for her. Chad was an only child. Shortly after his birth, his dad and she had separated. Brian worked for DARPA. As such, once he got onto one of their projects, he would not come home for days. He could not balance family life with his work. Besides that, he could not or would not share his work with her. Whether it was top secret or not, he hid it behind that title. That was his excuse. Finally, she filed for divorce. The courts gave her full custody of Chad. Then, the two of them moved west. Dad was now on one side of the US and mom on the other. The child support payments gave enough for them to survive. Brian made an excellent income. Lily cleaned for several wealthy residents around the Bay Area to supplement this.

Ten o'clock came and went. There was still no Chad. She was beside herself when she received a call from him. His water-proof cell phone case had not kept all of the salt water out of the inside workings, so it took some time to dry out. The signal finally returned.

Rex had taken him from the kitchen to a lab. It was hard for him to realize this miniature race of beings had tiny computers with massive power. The keyboards were too small for the giant's fingers to operate, but they had remarkable voice recognition capabilities.

"Hi, Mom. This is Chad. I won't be home tonight. "His mother reacted in an astonished voice.

"Why not? What happened? You

are not hurt, are you?"

"No, Mom, I am fine. I just have a project I need to finish. If I come home, it will put us way behind schedule."

"What kind of project? Is it something for school?"

"No, I have been hired to do some work for someone."

"Who hired you, Chad," she asked as she sat in her special chair?

"I have been hired by a government agency to do important work for them. Several lives are in danger. I must get to work on it immediately."

"It is not DARPA, is it, son?"

"No, Mother, but it is an agency, something like that. I am still determining how long it will take. I could be gone for a week or more. It just depends." Lily's fears were now confirmed. She knew deep down inside one day this would happen. The government could not allow geniuses like her husband and son to live everyday lives among the populace. They didn't belong in a normal society.

"What about school?"

"What about it? There is nothing they can teach me. It is boring me to death, and I do not fit in. The other kids pay no attention to me. It is as if I am not even there. Besides, after I complete this, millions of dollars will be made in new technologies that will soon hit the markets. In a few months, I will make enough money that you will never have to work another day. I will be home Monday and tell you all about it. You are not going to believe what happened." With that, the phone cut off. Mom tried to call him back, but there was no answer.

The Sea-Surrogates had been known as the Nomads before they started delving into the cloning process of creating a freshwater version of their kind using the earth dwellers. Their circulatory system would not allow them to survive in fresh water, but their counterparts could. Unlike the ones from within the land mass, they had gills and fins like fish. The saltwater was a strong conductor of electricity, whereas the inland lakes and streams were not. They found that if their citizens' incubation class carried the budding babies of the earthlings, they often developed gills, but not always. Unlike their masters, this altered race could harvest the resources from the inland bodies of water. Just as humans crave seafood, so did Rex's race of beings. It made up a large portion of their diet. To answer the question, did the beings thus created have souls? Yes, they did, but they no longer had free choice. Their life of existence was forced upon them. They were slaves. Those beings that did not have gills were forced to do other tasks for the race of sea dwellers. Once Chad was informed of the slave colonies, he set his mind to fight against them; no beings, whoever or whatever they were, should be enslaved. However, he did not share his views with Rex or his kind. He kept his beliefs to himself. Part of his work was to establish free will for the enslaved.

"I will need living specimens of all the races of Electronoyds, and I will be developing vaccines for Rex. It would be best if they were unaware they were being tested. Do your kind and your water rivals ever sleep or take some downtime to recharge? If so, is there a way to keep them in a state of downtime for an extended period of time? "Rex pondered the question before answering."

"Yes, we do require downtime to recharge. Forcing someone to be your test sample would violate their free will, and we cannot allow that. However, many sympathize with all races and will gladly submit to your experimentation if they feel it is for the greater good. I will have volunteers here in the lab within the next few hours."

"Is there anything else you feel you need to get started?"

"Yes, although you say your means of reproduction is asexual, you also mentioned that your ruler is a Matriarch. That would indicate you have a female counterpart to women in our race. What, if any, are the differences in the physical or electrical makeup of all beings in your race?"

"We have different sexes in our breeding system, as do the Sea Surrogates. The counterparts of your women are like your ladies. Their circulatory system is based on a negative charge, while their male counterparts have a positive electrical current passing through their circulatory makeup. We have one form of being you do not have, although your political system has recently been pushing a neutral form of humanity. In your world, these would be called transgender in nature. Our people are not the same; they are surrogates who bring new beings into our population like our water rivals. These counterparts to your transsexuals have a neutral current in their circulatory system, neither negative nor positive. That is how they can provide a safe incubation chamber for the new lives once our male and female kind choose to bond. Now you understand how this all happened. The race in the sea took the negative and positive components designed to create a new individual, and instead of our surrogates spawning them, their surrogates provided the place where the new life grew and developed before being brought into the world. You will need six volunteers from both races unless you plan to create something for the freshwater hybrids. I understand that a hybrid race of freshwater nomads has not been completed. I have not heard of any freshwater surrogate mothers. It is like when a horse and donkey mate in your world. A mule is formed but does not have the means to reproduce more of its kind. This gives me an idea that we need to discuss with Her Majesty. If you have the means and desire to free those enslaved and have them become their own race, then you might need to figure out how to develop a freshwater surrogate species to complete their cycle. Do you think you are up to all of this? There are a lot of unknowns, at least from my standpoint." The kid genius was allowing his photographic mind to search all the possibilities. He wanted to free those enslaved, but did they want to be free? Were they incapable of free will? Had that been bread out of them? He would only know this after he interviewed the volunteers.

"Did I hear you express doubt in my abilities to complete the task you have given me, Rex?"

"No, the only doubt I had was, could you create a freshwater surrogate, thus providing the elements necessary to form a new race of Electronoids as you have labeled us?"

"That is a good assumption. I do not know if it is possible. I am working in the dark here. You are the only Electro-humanoid I have been in contact with. I assume you are speaking the truth, that millions of your kind exist in this world, but until I meet others and check them out, I will not know what possibilities await us in this adventure. Will your seafaring counterparts volunteer also, and if so, will they need some special treatment since their habitat is the sea while yours is the earth?"

"Many among them are as concerned about this upcoming encounter with the humans as we are. If our cause can be presented in the right light, they will gladly volunteer any resources to help us. As for the freshwater hybrids, I have no idea how that will unfold."

Chapter 5

The Fate of Two Races

Chad was directed to sit before meeting the council of five. It comprised the Matriarch, Defense Minister, Chief Physicist, Chief Physician, and Top Scientist. A chair from the world above had been brought into the lab. He would be comfortable, at least. Rex recommended that he sit since a person of such immense proportions might intimidate someone. It was not like this Council of Five had never had contact with humans before. No, they had been observing them ever since they appeared in America. But to be up close and personal might be a new experience for some. The Matriarch was the oldest of the five or seven now, since Rex and himself was invited into the council. She had had dealings with these humans and their government in the past. This was how some of the many legends of races of people below the surface of the earth had their beginning. It would not be a problem for her. But the Physicist was new to them. He had teleported in from the other side of the world. It was because of his brilliance he had come. Minds like his were few and far between, even among this little race. Likewise, the Physician understood, like no other person in this group, the workings of the Electro-humanoids. His knowledge would be invaluable to Chad and the task he was set to perform. Finally, they emerged from beyond the vale. Somebody had brought in six chairs and a table. They took their seats behind it. Rex gave the introductions.

"Madam, Matriarch, meet Chad, the one we have been preparing for this encounter. He has agreed to our terms. Chad, meet Madam, Matriarch, Her Majesty, Glorietta. She will be persuading over this meeting." The Matriarch bowed her head in recognition. Not knowing what to do, Chad returned the bow. Next, the Defense Minister was introduced as Sir Neptune. He was followed by the Chief Physician, who went by the name of Sir Ratcliff. The Physicist followed. His name was more common. He was called Sir John the Great. The Top Scientist was a woman again if this counterpart to the race above had women. She was as beautiful as she was small. Her features were a picture of perfection. Chad developed a crush on her the moment she entered the door. She went by the name of Madam Starlight. The kid genius bowed his head momentarily for each of them as they were introduced, even as they did to him. Then, the Matriarch called the meeting to order.

"We have met here under these unusual circumstances to consider the events unfolding around us. The fate of two races of beings, possibly three, is at stake. Grave things are happening to all our worlds. The leaders of the sea dwellers are set on eliminating humans from the equation. They are polluting their habitat to a point of toxicity that threatens to destroy the place that has been their home for thousands of years. Likewise, those of us who dwell on the land are feeling the effects of these poisons as they keep leaching into the ground. At the rate they are going, even our race will be marked for extension. Then, there is the slave race that threatens our very morals. This young man has agreed to help us resolve these imminent threats to all our worlds. We have selected him because he possesses a keen mind that the human educational system has not compromised. He has not yet been discovered by the human elite. We got to him before they did. We are happy to be working in partnership with you Sir, Chad. Already, we have heard of some ideas you have put forward to help those enslaved and bring an end to their master's goals. Thank you." Chad was impressed by the little lady's speech. She was very composed and showed utmost respect to him. Not many had done this in his short 15 years of life. It felt good.

"Thank you for putting your faith in me, your Majesty. With the help of all of you, I believe our endeavors to work toward a solution to these many problems can be accomplished. Some things must be worked out, but with your minds working together to accomplish this, I know we will be successful. Thank you for bringing me into your world. It has been an adventure so far that I will never forget." And that would be a true statement coming from Chad indeed, for he seldom forgot anything.

The meeting lasted for the better part of an hour. Time within was on a slightly different cycle than in the world without. They divided their waking and recharging time into thirds. For two-thirds of the time, they carried on their everyday activities. The remaining third of the time was spent in rest. The Physician educated Chad on all the mechanical workings of the smaller race of beings. It was more elementary than the complicated biological processes in the human body. If one could carefully observe, it would appear that the androids now making their way into human life above were patterned after these little people living in their own world for so long below the earth's crust in an alternate dimension.

They provided him with a meal. Some of their own had gone into the upper strata and brought back a meal in a bag from McDonalds. It had all his favorite food, including the chicken burger he had always ordered when going there. Then he rested. On the marrow, the volunteers arrived and were brought into the lab. There appeared to be no fear in their assessment of him or the fact they would be a sort of guinea pig for the upcoming electronic vaccines. The ocean dwellers could survive out of their habitat for several days as they could exist underwater and in the open. They would not need to be placed in a seawater tank. This was good news.

All the volunteers were not in favor of a war with humanity. They were happy to help in any way possible. It had taken some doing to get some freshwater hybrids to come. These made up the largest number of volunteers. Some had fins and gills, some had one or the other, and others had no gills or fins at all. If they had no soul, it was not apparent. Each came with a unique personality, even one similar to that of humans. It was a lively bunch that gladly extended an arm or leg to the Physician as he drew the samples from them. If they experienced any pain, they did not reveal it. Chad wondered if they felt anything at all. There were emotions expressed even as in his world. Some female counterparts would tear up as they heard of the work the freshwater volunteers were forced to do. Then there was laughter. The jokes flew around the group fluently, and everyone joined in the laughter. They were a jolly bunch most of the time. Chad would have loved to have laughed, but the volume of his vocal cords would have shaken things up too much, so he just smiled or grinned, nodding his head when he caught the punch line. Finally, with a lot of help, the vaccines were developed. It was time to test them on willing subjects.

Chapter 6

The Birth of A Fairy

It took exactly one week to develop and test the vaccines on thousands of volunteers. In case of possible side effects, perhaps even death, a program was created that uploaded the pre-shot state of the volunteers to a quantum computer. It served as an antidote if things got out of hand. They could be restored to their former state. It was a good thing they put this precaution into effect. The first vaccination caused close to 30% of the volunteers to grow unusual-looking crystals in their brains. There were certain areas in the world within that amplified the electromagnetic pulses they tapped into for power. If a vaccinated individual passed through these highly charged areas, the crystals in the brain would vibrate with the frequency of the surroundings and cause what one might describe as a brain bleed. Since the little ones were nearly transparent, it was easy to spot this side effect. Unlike humans, who have red blood flowing through their veins, the beings within had a purple fluid that passed through their circulatory system. You could not see the fluid as long as there were no ruptures in their veins. But in their brain, when the bleed came, you could see the veins and the fluid bleed out. The council took several who developed this side effect into observation. Depending on the strength of the vibrations, they could survive for up to two weeks before it was lethal enough to kill them. Once they found out the time frame of this, any who developed aneurysms were immediately returned to their pre-vaccination state. These aneurysms were not painful. The ones developing them felt nothing. Those from the sea who received this injection suffered no consequences or side effects from this inoculation. So, after several tests.

This was found to be effective in those ocean dwellers who wished not to be a part of the upcoming war.

Another side effect of this vaccine was that some volunteers started developing holes in their bodies. This did not cause death because the circulation moved around the holes. Let me give you an example. Imagine a donut. You have probably eaten one or two in your life. Now, in several donuts, there is a hole in the middle. That does not hurt the donut; there is just less to eat. The dough goes around the hole. This will give you an idea of what happened to some of the little ones within. You could see right through the hole. Several developed holes in what would be the lung areas in humans. One little miss developed a hole right through her head. It was at the top of her forehead, just about where the hairline would be if they had hairline, and gave her the odd appearance of a cyclops. It may have looked like hair in these little ones, but it was the same material the rest of their body was

bit of rivalry to their everyday humor. As Chad watched, he was genuinely amazed. Life would be much better if people could behave like these little creatures. There would not be fights or other instances where people got hurt. If a volunteer got bent out of shape by the vaccination, no matter what they looked like, there was no racism targeted at them.

The 'Translucents' had a heart of sorts. It regulated the flow of electrons in their little bodies. Every portion of these creatures needed constant charging to keep them alive. Their body was composed of a liquid promoting electrical charge flow. Perhaps the worst of the side effects was the failure of this organ to carry on its designated responsibility. From a human standpoint, we would label what happened to them as a heart attack. This organ simply quit doing what it was supposed to or started acting out of harmony with the other organs. Some would clog up. Sometimes, the negative or positive charges would bunch up and stall the circulation. A saline solution could be injected, and sometimes, it would bring the system back to order. This proved the most difficult for Chad and the council to address. But after trying several solutions, they found a remedy or remedies. Still, some of the volunteers did not like gambling with this uncertainty.

A small percentage of the volunteers lost their sense of smell. This was deadly. It was necessary for these ones from within to have a keen sense of smell. Though they appeared to live in a different world altogether, toxins from the humans seeping into the soil could kill large numbers of these humanoids. Without smell, they could not avoid passing through the toxic areas because they could not smell the foul orders that reeked around such areas. Several of the carriers of the new little ones soon to be born aborted the tiny ones growing inside. This caused great sadness. These 'Translucents,' did not see the babies that came about through their asexual reproduction process as nothing. They were real little, little ones and had as much of a right to life as the rest. Unfortunately, no treatment was developed to bring these little ones back from their fate. By realizing the power of this, Chad could have created the vaccination further to cause the Sea Surrogates to become infertile. When the realization of this came over him, he felt the power surge through him. Lesser men than he would not have been able to resist this power they could weld over the masses. Chad was not power-hungry, though, so he was not tempted by this.

There was a fortunate aspect to this infertility factor. However, it was the key to making it possible for the race from the sea to not be able to raise the budding young within their sea surrogates. He headed over to the electron microscope to have a closer look. There was a difference in the electrical charge of the two races. The earth's dwelling inhabitants had a current that operated like a modern alternating current, which was used in most instances. The electrical charge alternated from negative to positive at speeds that were too great to monitor with their equipment. The surrogate's current was two positive pulses for every negative one.

The sea dwellers had a current that did two short positive and two short negative bursts. In the males, the bursts were shorter than in the females. It was strange to Chad when he realized that, unlike humans, both the male and female species could create new buds, resulting in life. The males could only create male babies, and the females could only create female babies. When the male and female came together in intercourse, it was typically to regulate and balance the electrical impulses in each. If a female went too long without intimacy, her more negative charge could get even more negative. That would not happen, though, unless she were isolated. If she was out spouting too powerful of a negative charge, the males could not resist, and the two would have the interchange necessary to bring things back into balance. Likewise, if the males were separated for too long a period from the females, their drive was very powerful, and they found it hard to keep away from the ladies until those needs were met. Now, when a super positive charged male copulated with a super negative charged female, both would produce offspring shortly afterward, but they would usually come out to be the surrogate host from the race within.

The young genius segregated a substance that produced three positive charges for every negative one and added it to the vaccination solution. One little guy wanted to set the record for having the most injections. He had been returned to normal no less than seven times when things went wrong. He was called and told what this would do. This new injection should not affect the residents of the world within; only the sea-dwelling neighbors would be affected. He was injected and put in a holding room where he could be observed more closely. He liked going to this place because the fruit quota given to residents there was much higher for those who received the test vaccinations, and he loved fruit very much. After 24 hours of feasting on choice fruit, he was released. There were no effects. If he created a bud baby, no sea surrogate could raise it to maturity in their womb. This was finally a successful vaccination for these little ones. Meanwhile, with the extension in time, more side effects from the first vaccination showed up.

It happened to a person of promise, Sarah Lea. Of all those who had participated, she held the most promise. She was a medalist, you might say, in their equivalent to our Olympics. She had the body of a nymph and could do everything faster and better than anyone else. During an extensive energy output one day, her circulation system simply clotted up and stopped. She turned into a transparent sculpture of an unknown makeup. Had someone from the world

without stumbled upon her, she would have appeared as a miniature, intricate likeness of a human female made out of glass or transparent plastic. In Sarah's case, bringing her back to life was impossible. The council needed a deceased body to recharge. Though she had a body, there was no way to recharge her. She was the first beloved victim to die in this way. Later, the same thing happened to another dozen, especially active creatures. Taking a small biopsy to the microscope revealed that she had undergone a chemical transformation into an entirely new element that was not in any periodic table. Chad named it Sarachrysalis after the beloved athlete.

Another 17 test subjects became quadriplegic with some autoimmune disorder where their bodies started attacking themselves. These had to be rebooted to get them back to normal. In still another 20 cases, the victim's bodies began to liquidate rather than solidify, as in the case of Sarah Lea.

When this happened, internal organs lost the ability to hold together under activity. Typically, the minds of these little ones within were very sharp. In nearly half of the subjects, a form of mindless dementia developed. You would find them wandering around, not knowing where they were going. These were taken back and rebooted, which would, in most cases, return them to their jolly selves again. A percentage of them developed multiple side effects from the vaccination. This never resulted in any good to the volunteers.

In time, a memorial service was planned for Sarah Lea. Thousands turned out. It was a somber occasion. They had her in a glass casket. Many of her friends got up and testified about how she had influenced them. However, a little one noticed movement within the casket about three-quarters of the way through the service. The lady within opened her eyes and raised her hand up to the top of the glass. Then, as she felt the enclosure, she panicked. She started thrashing around frantically. They had dressed her in a violate robe with golden lace. Her medals were all around her neck. Finally, the Matriarch commanded to open the top and let her out. The moment she was exposed to the air, a transformation occurred. She developed shimmering, gold wings. A type of metamorphosis had transformed her into a fairy goddess. Chad had never seen such a beautiful creature in his life. When she spoke, her voice had also transformed and was very musical. If he had never believed in fairies, he would have been a believer now, for that is what she was. She produced a small vial of violate liquid from a pocket in her gown.

"Greetings, dwellers from within; I hold in my hand that magic formula necessary to end all of our problems with the race of sea nymphs. One must sneak into the central hub of the water dwellers and release it where the water spouts move upward and outward in all directions. It will unite with the water in these circulation chambers and transform them into a negative, negative polarity. In the future, anytime the water vortexes are used, those using them will be returned to a neutral electrical phase. War will never happen between our races. We will continue to trade with them as we have for centuries. I will not be able to deliver this. I suggest that the human, Chad, be appointed to do this. He alone has the means to accomplish it in his possession. In the meantime, I have been given great wisdom. After today, you must appoint me to the council. There will be drastic changes soon in our world. We all will need to work together, or this habitation we are all a part of will be gone forever." With these closing words, Sarah Lea took to the air and flew away. Her robes and wings were shimmering with glory. She became luminescent, changing from one color to another until they lost sight of her.

Chapter 7

The Bubble that Changed Everything

Chad and the fabulous minds working with him could not develop a method to create the much-needed Surrogate for the freshwater hybrids. True to his word, he returned to the world without where his mother eagerly waited for him. With him, he carried the precious vial. He had a great reunion with his mom. Several hugs were exchanged between them. She had felt the significant loss of her husband and now that of her son. It had been hard on her. He had not communicated with her since the phone call. Every waking minute had been devoted to their cause. Now, his mind needed a break. Any genius knows this. Much of what they conger up comes when their mind is occupied with other things than the task at hand. It was no different with Chad. He refused to think through the problem they faced. It would not be productive. In time, during a moment of recognition, the solution would come. He even decided to venture back to school. Something happened to him last week. He had matured in human relationships. He had never worked with a team of great minds like his own before. It had been invigorating, to say the least. He viewed all humans from a completely different perspective now. They were polluting their environment to the point of destruction, yet none seemed aware. It was sad. His last class was chemistry. The teacher confronted him about his absence from class for the previous week. Chad only smiled. He did not enter into an argument with his teacher.

"You are flunking this class, Chad, and I know this is not you. You are not even trying to live up to your potential. You have a brilliant mind. I fear you are wasting it on nonsense. Let me make a proposal to you. If you can share something with the class today that will wow me and them, I will take that F and put another leg on it." The rest of the class were all in on this challenge. For the first time they actually noticed this new student that entered their ranks. Many were smirking. They did not think he could wow anyone. "Remember, Chad. I am giving you one chance to walk away with an A for the entire year. Are you up to the challenge?" Chad's smile grew broader. He remembered the Polarscoptic Resonator in his pocket. He did not want them to see the jeweled case, so he opened it in his pants and pulled out the little scope. He held it up for all to see.

"This has occupied my time for the last week, Mr. Brown. It has some chemical properties that have been altered, enabling it to do some amazing things. You are aware of the principle behind making bubbles with soap, are you not?" His teacher nodded, and several of the students did, too. They had been studying the process that

of soap to see who could create the bubble that lasted the longest before bursting. Ken held the record at that very moment and Gertrude was a close second. She held the record for blowing the largest bubble. She now watched Chad with great interest as if she had second thoughts about leaving him stunned at the table a little over a week ago. Chad gave her a wink and continued with his little speech. "I, too, have been working with this." He closed his finger around the scope and showed it to everyone present. A thin film like that of the rings of the bubble soap formed on the inside, much to everyone's amazement. "The substance inside this tube is more concentrated than any soap you have worked with. It will create a bubble of massive proportions." Several students started laughing. That was not possible to do. Chad would keep his F, they were certain. "Let me demonstrate it to you." Following Rex's instructions, he made a circle of each hand around the tube. In place of one bubble, two formed.

There was one a little ways back from each end. He held it up for all to see again, then, putting it to his mouth, began to blow. A bubble formed and grew larger and larger. He had to take several breaths. Each one increased in size until, finally, it was larger than he was. It was time. He stepped inside. The bubble closed all around him. He was looking out from the world within. The class was astonished! They could see Chad inside waving at them. The teacher grabbed his cell phone and took pictures from several angles. Several of the students did the same. This would be top news in the student paper on Monday. Chad waved at them all one more time. Then there was a boom. It was not loud enough to break any windows, but it shook things up in the lab. Several test tubes and glass equipment fell to the floor and shattered. Where Chad had been standing, there was nothing. The kid genius, the bubble, the little tube, were all gone. They simply vanished.

Chad found himself in a large

room beneath what appeared to be the sea. He was in a bubble much like the one that had popped in the classroom. He found it rotated like the wheel guinea pigs used in their cages. It went in whatever direction he directed. There was another element of surprise. The bubble he was in went through things as if they were not even there. He entered another door. It was a lab. Several sea dwellers were working on implanting bonded electro cells within their surrogate hosts. He was able to move around unnoticed, uninhibited, and observe everything. He followed one being out a door and went to another room. Inside that one, several of their earth-dwelling neighbors were being forced to bond. The slave masters were harvesting the cellular buds that formed from these unions.

The young man grew furious as he watched. This must stop! There had to be a way. He continued to roll around in this environment for half an hour, checking things out. Finally, he saw how they brought the captives to the chamber. There was a door not unlike the one he had passed through to enter the little room with the fireplace. On the other side was a tunnel. The victims came in containers. The sea dwellers were a bit larger than those on the land. Their electrical current was more substantial. They were using these means to force or attract their prey to follow them. They had no choice against such attraction. They were drawn to it like a magnet. At that instant, it all came together. He knew how to stop this slave colony. He only needed to weaken the electrical circulatory system surging through the Sea-Surrogates so that it could no longer overpower their weaker neighbors. It would also take the spark out of them that was fueling a future war with the humans above. This process could be administered through the substance he had prepared for them back in the lab. These beings would not accept the vaccine without good reason, so there would need to be another means of administration.

Further out in the ocean, Chad came to the spout hub. Several water spouts shot out of the ocean and entered the heavens. These must be the transport system the sea dwellers in this area used to move about the planet. The earth dwellers had a similar system of travel that could propel them instantly from point to point. Through this system of water tunnels the genius would inoculate the unsuspecting race. He would inject these travel ways with the substance prepared for them from the vial. It would permeate them like a computer virus. In time, all who traveled these waterways way would be infected. These, intern would infect others. There would be a massive pandemic. Should he do it now? As he pondered the situation, the little vial seemed to glow brighter and brighter. It was signaling him to do it. He worked the little cap open and watched in wonder as an array of rainbow colors swirled up into each vortex. It was the most beautiful thing he had witnessed aside

from the fairy and the scientist he had developed a crush on. When it was all dispersed, he still waited.

What should he do now? Rex had not told him how to reverse the effect of the bubble. He decided to experiment. If blowing on the tube caused the bubble to form in the first place, perhaps drawing air into the device would have the opposite reaction. It was worth a try. The lad withdrew it from its case and, placing the fingers of both hands in position, watched as the lenses formed again at either end. He put it to his mouth and gently began to inhale. It worked. The bubble became smaller and smaller. Then, it collapsed upon itself and returned to the scope. Chad found himself on the earth's surface back in the world without. He was on the football field. The students had long since gone home. Slowly, he made his way to the house. It was time to initiate phase two.

Now, it is time for readers to answer some questions. Do you feel it is right for people like Chad to force their agenda upon unwilling subjects if it is for the greater good? If your answer is yes, how do these individuals determine what the greater good is? The world faced a pandemic of global proportions in 2020. There were people behind it all with a particular agenda in mind. They were determined to carry it out no matter the cost. Did they have the right to do this? If so, who gave them that right?

How should Chad and the council of seven carry out their mission from this point on? It might be good to discuss your answers with others. See what you come up with. Also, is it right to do experimental genetic manipulation on the unsuspecting masses even if some council of seven somewhere in the world determines it is for the greater good?

THE END

www.ingramcontent.com/pod-product-compliance
Lightning Source LLC
Chambersburg PA
CBHW070355310726
48977CB00002B/450